A BHS Tall Story Book

An Adventure for
Hannah
Hippo

A BHS **Tall Story Book**

An Adventure for Hannah Hippo

Written and illustrated by Douglas Hall

This edition produced exclusively for

BHS
LONDON

Hannah overheard her
Mummy say to her
neighbour Mrs Giraffe,
"I must go and pick some
blackberries to make
blackberry jam.
I do like it on brown
bread and butter."

Hannah was going to visit her Grannie that afternoon and she decided that on the way back she would pick some blackberries for her Mummy.

"Hello Grannie Hippo. I've
brought your favourite flowers
and a jar of Mummy's
homemade strawberry jam.
I hope you like it."

"Oh, I shall, I shall," replied Grannie. "There is nothing I like so much as a little strawberry jam on brown bread and butter for my tea."

On the way home
Hannah stopped by
the hedgerow to pick
some blackberries.
She soon had a bagful.
There was one big juicy
blackberry at the end
of a branch and Hannah
tried to reach it.

But she slipped and fell
– SPLASH! – into the river.
   There were some fishermen
on the bank and they
fell off their little stools
with laughter.
   Poor, wet, Hannah.

But one of the fishermen
was kind and helped her out
of the water.

"It's a funny way to feed
the fish — with blackberries!
Here's a couple of fish for
you to take home for tea.
They are lovely with a bit
of brown bread and butter."

"I'm sorry about the blackberries, but I am pleased that you are all right," said Mummy when Hannah got home. "Let's get you some dry clothes to put on, then I'll cook for you the fish that the kind fisherman gave to you."

"Mummy," said Hannah.

"Yes, dear."

"We could have one each. They will be lovely for tea with a little bit of brown bread and butter."

And they were!

This edition first published exclusively for
British Home Stores plc in 1986
by The Hamlyn Publishing Group Limited
London · New York · Sydney · Toronto
Bridge House, 69 London Road, Twickenham, Middlesex TW1 3SB, England

Text and illustrations Copyright © Deans International Publishing,
a division of The Hamlyn Publishing Group Limited, 1986

ISBN 0 603 00824 0

Printed and bound by Purnell Book Production Ltd.,
Paulton,
Bristol.
Member of BPCC plc